HOUSE GUESTS 101

NANCY LINE

Acknowledgement:

I would like to thank all of these people and animals that have inspired me to write this book.

- God
- Richard
- Brigite
- Brett
- Chantal
- Lori
- Beth
- Meg
- Sussanah
- Fran
- Sue
- Phil
- LG
- Jamie
- Kevin
- Lorrae
- Rocco

Introduction:

For nearly three decades, my husband and I led a busy life raising two children while tending to our family business in Northern Virginia. When the children left the nest, we sought a simpler, warmer life, so we began to spend our winters in Naples, Florida.

By that point in my life, I finally had the time to turn to my life's passion --writing. But what would I write? Little did I know that spending endless winters in Florida with unexpected house guests would provide me with the fodder for this book and spark a new chapter in my life.

As admitted snowbirds, we embraced the Florida lifestyle and became avid golf and tennis players. These hobbies encouraged us to open our home to friends from near and far and from all walks of life.

Being a very generous guy with many buddies, Richard, my husband, always said, "Come on down" to his friends. So, as the days up north grew shorter and the temperature dropped, we miraculously would receive holiday cards and phone calls from people we hadn't seen in years. These "friends" would hint for an invite, or in some cases, invite themselves down to our home for extended periods of time.

The names on these pages are fictitious to protect our friends and guests' reputations (and unusual habits). But they'll know who they are when they read their story. It's been a joy to share these memories and has kept me laughing non-stop.

I hope these stories brighten your day.

CHAPTERS

01

TYPES OF GUESTS

02

GOLFING HOUSE GUESTS

03

DO'S AND DON'TS FOR HOUSE GUESTS

04

EXCUSES TO KEEP HOUSE GUESTS AWAY

You know what they say about fish and house guests.....after 3 days.

Have you ever noticed that there are many types of people, just like in the animal kingdom?

1

TYPES OF GUESTS

YOU KNOW YOU ARE IN TROUBLE WHEN...

1.
JOE WITH THE TOES

"This Florida sunshine really makes my toe nails grow like crazy." "Oh, can you tell the maid to vacuum my room?"

2.
RACHEL THE CAT HATER

"I HATE CATS!"
"Don't you have any Benadryl?" "This cat will
destroy your furniture."
The cat urinated in the woman's suitcase and began
to purr.

3.
SASSY: THE CLOTHES HORSE

"I bought so many clothes, may I borrow one of your suitcases?"

4.
JOE THE CHEAPO

"Oh my God, I forgot my wallet, can you spot me on this one?" "I will pick up dinner the next time that I visit."

5.
WANDA, THE WINE MONSTER

"We're out of wine, I'm having a panic attack." "You should stock up on beverages."

6.
GARY WITH GAS

"Excuse me, those beans that you cooked are a problem, I will chase them with a beer." "Oh no, we're out of beer."

7.
MARK THE SHARK

"Can you pick me up at the airport?
"These cab rides cost a fortune?"

8.
EILEEN THE QUEEN

"I don't know how to operate your washer and dryer." "I sure don't want to break them."

9.
PAUL THE BROTHER-IN-LAW

"Maybe I can change my flight and stay longer."
"I love to spend time with family."
"See you the same time next year."

10.
TOM DROPS THE BOMB

"I need a plunger, these paper towels won't flush."
"You should pick up some good toilet paper at Costco."

11.
VEGAN MEGAN

"I'm a vegan, don't you have some tofu
turkey?"
"How could you kill that poor bird?"

12.
CHUCK WITH THE PUPS

"My dogs are trained and would never
have an accident."
"It must be your dog."

13.
ALWAYS LATE NATE

"I missed my flight, and it's freezing in New York, may I stay another week?"

14.
ADAIR WITH THE HAIR

"The maid can clean up this mess."

15.
RUDY THE FOODY

"They sure don't make furniture like they used to."

16.
LAZY HAZEL

"We can clean up later, let's go shopping."

17.
LILLIAN THE LIZARD

"Your house is too big, you should down-
size."

18.
RON MR. MOM

"Everyone out of the pool, the baby's diaper came off." "Oops, and we are out of diapers."

19.
DOUBLE DIPPING DEBBIE

"Love your chili con queso."
"Here, have some."
"I don't want to be a pig."

20.
GUY WITH BAD EYES

"Can you drive, I can't see at night?"
"Your car gets better gas mileage than mine."

21.
REALLY RALPH

"Your car sure burns the gasoline, I only
went to the beach 6 times." "What a gas
hog!"

22.
SICK VICK

"I must have picked up a bug on the plane, hope you don't come down with this."
"Do you have any meds that I can take?"

23.
GUZZLING GUS

"Milk really builds healthy bones."
"They have 2 for one at Publix."

24.
NEAL THE CEREAL KILLER

He didn't realize that he was eating out of the cat's bowl. He poured a second bowl.

25.
HOWARD IN THE SHOWER

"Singing in the Rain."
He used all of the hot water.

26.
FRUGAL FRED

"You will love to hang out with these guys, they are a blast."
"They can sleep on the floor in your room."

27.
JANET FROM ANOTHER PLANET

"OMG what happened?"
"I only used a little."

28.
NATE AFTER MY PLATE

"Your dinner looks so much better than mine, may I have a bite?"

29.
FANCY NANCY

"Do I look fat in this size zero bathing
suit?"
"You should try the keto diet."

JOYCE WITH THE VOICE

"I really don't enjoy sports."
"Can you change the channel?"

2

GOLFING HOUSE GUESTS:

31.
JAKE VERSUS THE LAKE

"I paid big bucks for this club and it's not helping my game one bit." "Grrrrr."

32.
SLY GUY

"Oh, I hit a great shot after all."

33.
PAT WITH POOR MATH

"Wow, I shot a 44 today."
"I was on fire."

34.
LOUD ALF

"You're going to hook it to the left again, just like you did last time."

35.
KNOW IT ALL SAUL

"You're not keeping your head down, you
need a golf lesson."

36.
SLOW MOE

**" It's going to be midnight, by the time
we finish this round."**

37.
FRAN THE SPEED DEMON

**"Hold on." Haha
"I love driving a golf cart."**

38.
SHOW OFF SANDY

"I think golf is so easy."
"In fact, I got 7 holes in one last year."
(She really did achieve this.)

39.
RON THE CON MAN

"Want to bet five dollars a hole?"
"I haven't played in months."

40.
ROGER THE SAND BAGGER

"I have a 33 handicap, but somehow I shot an 84 today."

41.
THE ONE AND ONLY KENNY

"I love this grapefruit juice." "Oops, I spilled it in your Baby Grande." "Wish I had a piano like this."

42.
HUNGRY HANK

"Wow, we just had breakfast, and I am
already hungry again." "What time are
you serving lunch today?"

43.
CIGAR TIME

"I love these Cuban cigars that you bought." "Nothing like a good cigar after taking your money at golf."

44.
FAST FOOD EDDIE

"I'm treating for dinner tonight."
"What fast food restaurant do you prefer?"
"We can split a meal."

45.
SNEAKY PETE

"We will be in Florida next week."
"All of the hotels are booked."
"Would love to see you."

46.
MUSICAL MIKE

**"I just love the oldies, especially Frankie
Valli."**
"You're just too good to be true."

47.
RUTHIE

**"I hope that you don't mind me teeing up
my ball
on the fairway, it is much easier."**

48.
SEARCHING SAM

"There are so many nice golf balls in the lake,"
"I just found twelve."
"Oh, it's my turn to hit."

49.
NOSEY NICK

"Hey, what club did you use on that shot?"
"I see that your ball landed in the sand
again."

50.
GET A LIFE LLOYD

"These practice swings really loosen me up."
"That's how Greg Norman warms up."

51.
BATTLE OF THE SEXES.....RICH AND LOLA

**"Double or nothing Lola, you'll never get that ball
on the green."**

BONUS PAGE.
BEING POPULAR IN FLORIDA

"I didn't know that we had so many friends."

3

DO'S AND DON'TS FOR HOUSE GUESTS:

Do's

DO bring coffee, soft drinks, snacks, chocolate, good wine, etc.

DO offer to help with the cleaning.

DO pick up after yourself.

DO leave the bathroom the way you found it.

DO treat your hosts to at least one lunch or dinner.

DO send a thank you note upon returning to your home.

Don'ts

DON'T arrive early and stay later than planned.

DON'T come in empty handed.

DON'T drag your suit case across the wooden stairs.

DON'T complain about the weather.

DON'T track sand in the house.

DON'T use a new towel every day.

DON'T cheat at golf.

DON'T step on the cat.

DON'T let the pets out of the house.

4

**EXCUSES TO KEEP HOUSE
GUESTS AWAY:**

WEATHER TACTICS:

"I think an asteroid may be passing over this area."

"You won't believe it, but a cold front is coming and we could actually get some snow."

"Red tide alert for Florida."

"Those poor dead fish are on the beach, so don't forget your respirator."

ANIMAL TACTICS:

"Our cats have fleas, so watch your ankles."

"I am fostering two pit bulls all season."

"You can't be too safe with the crime rate here in Florida."

"I'm trying to break the dog's habit of biting people."

"A black bear has been sighted on our lanai. "It was actually swimming in our pool."

"These pythons are really beautiful."

"I saw one this morning with a small animal in its mouth."

"It's mating season for alligators and they can be vicious."

"A few days ago, an alligator pulled a woman's golf club from her hand." "Wish I had my camera with me."

"We found a nest of rats in the guest room, those baby mice are so precious."

"My husband just adopted a spider monkey from the Naples Zoo. "It loves to cuddle with our guests."

"I have volunteered to care for twelve toddlers from a pre-school. "I could sure use an extra hand changing all of these diapers."

"There are so many bad drivers in Florida." "Be careful, or they will run you down in a parking lot."

"Retirement is so boring." "I wish I were working again and commuting for 2 hrs a day."

"Sure come on down." "I have a torn rotator and I would be happy if you helped me clean the litter box for my 14 feral cats." "Don't forget to get your rabies shot."

OTHER TACTICS:

"There's a great hotel down the street."

"I'm turning our house into an Airbnb at only $200 per night."

"The traffic is really heavy here in the Sunshine State."

"You're so lucky to enjoy a change of seasons up north." "You can sit by the fireplace." "I do miss the cold winter and the beautiful snow."

"We always have bad hair days here, with such high humidity."

"Bring your sunscreen, this intense sunshine will damage your skin and make you look much older."

"Florida can be so boring."

"It's flu season, and I wouldn't advise anyone to board an airplane or even drive a car to Florida, especially at your age."

"The price of gasoline has hit an all-time high." "It's much cheaper, to spend the winter up north."

We will be going out for every meal, so bring your wallet."

"Aunt Hilda will be sharing the up-stairs with you." "She's such a 104-year-old joy."

"We will be conserving energy by turning the air conditioning off all season." "We have disconnected the television and we are enjoying, getting back to nature."

"I'm going on a two week fast, so I will not be cooking."
"Feel free to bring your own food."

DESPERATION TACTICS:

- Don't answer the phone or your emails.

- Change your phone number.

- Rent your Florida home and take a 3 month cruise.

HELPFUL HINTS:

- Hire a teenager to assist with the children or have her assist with the cleanup.

- Take the laundry to a laundromat.

- Have food delivered to your door.
- Use paper plates and plastic cutlery.
- Before the guests arrive, make sure that the duration of their stay fits your schedule.
- Suggest that the guests rent their own vehicle, or take a cab to and from the airport.

"Enjoy, You Know who you are."

Made in the USA
Columbia, SC
03 April 2021